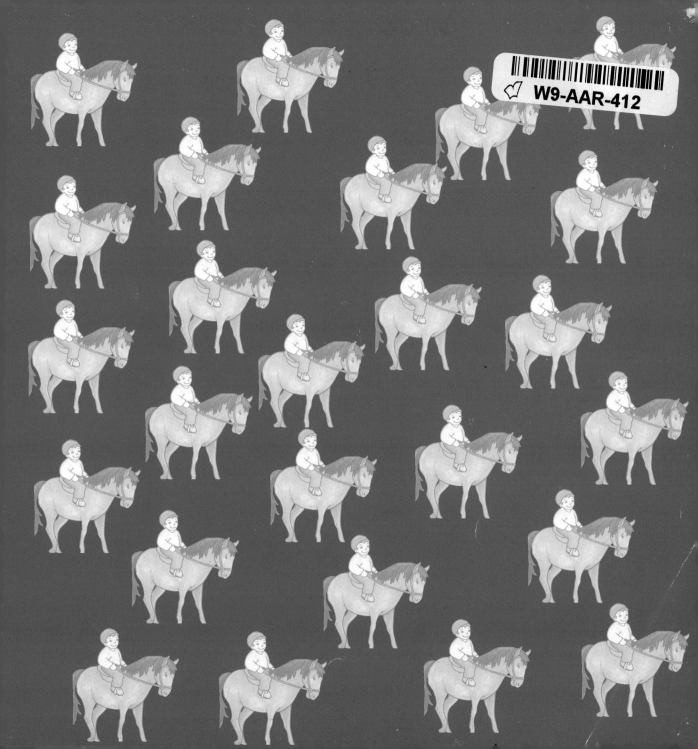

MUSLIM CHILDREN'S LIBRARY

Muslim Nursery Rhymes
Author Mustafa Yusuf McDermont
Cover/Book Design and Illustrator Terry Norridge-Austen

Published by The Islamic Foundation,
Markfield Conference Centre, Ratby Lane, Markfield,
Leicestershire LE67 9SY, United Kingdom
Email: publications@islamic-foundation.com,
Website: www.islamic-foundation.com

Quran House, PO Box 30611, Nairobi, Kenya

PMB 3193, Kano, Nigeria

Distributed by Kube Publishing Ltd.
Tel: +44(0)1530 249230, Fax: +440)1530 249656
Email: info@kubepublishing.com

British Library Cataloguing in Publication Data

McDermott, Mustafa Yusuf
Muslim nursery rhymes
1. Nursery rhymes - Pictorial works 2. Islamic poetry - Pictorial works
I.Title II. Norridge, Terry III. Islamic Foundation
398 .8'0917671

ISBN 978-0-86037-342-1

Printed by
IMAK Printing & Publishing, TURKEY

Muslim
Nursery Rhymes

Mustafa Yusuf McDermont

Illustrated by Terry Norridge-Austen

THE ISLAMIC FOUNDATION

1. Hush a Bye Baby

Hush a bye baby, so pure and small,
He created you, created us all.
Hush a bye baby, we've no need to fear,
We're never alone, when Allah's so near.

Hush a bye baby, breathing so calm,
He will protect us and keep us from harm.
Hush a bye baby, so still and serene,
You are a Muslim and Islam's your *Deen*.

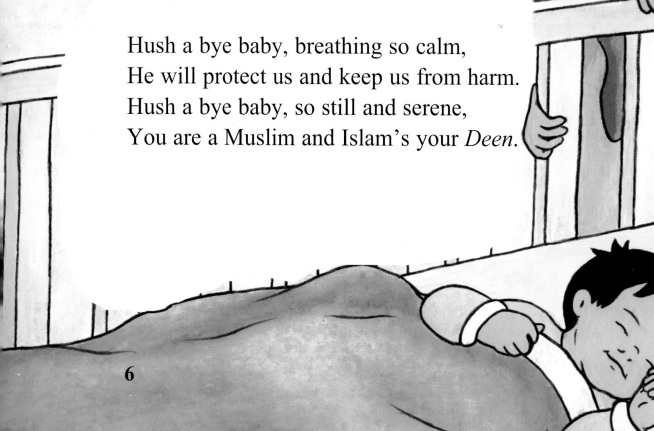

2. You are a Muslim

Rock a bye baby,
Your cradle is green.
You are a Muslim
And Islam's your *Deen*.
Allah's the Lord
His word is Qur'an.
Muhammad His Prophet,
Last Messenger to man.

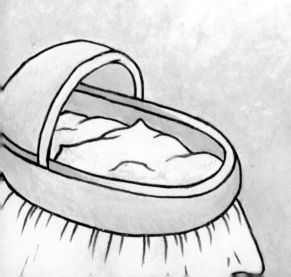

7

3. Silver Star

Brightly shining Silver Star,
Who has made you as you are?
Sparkling over land and sea,
High above the highest tree.

Allah created you and me
In truth so perfectly.

8

4. **Little Pony**

I had a little pony,
He wouldn't go anywhere,
Till he heard the *Muezzin*
Calling us to prayer.

Then clip-clop, clip-clop,
To the Mosque we'd go,
Summer and winter,
Sunshine or snow.

9

5. *Adhan*

Muhammad Hassan!
Muhammad Hassan!
Come call *Adhan*,
And bring all the Muslims to prayer.

Bring them from the factory,
Bring them from the school,
Bring them from their comfy bed
And from their easy chair.

10

Call them in the morning,
Call them in the night,
Call everyone to Islam
Call them to the light.

11

6. Boys and Girls

It's Time To Pray

Boys and girls it's time to pray,
Adhan is called five times a day.

Stop your playing or leave your sleep,
Ignore the noises in the street.

Pack up your toys and leave your games,
Remember Allah, Most Glorious of names.

Come in a hurry, come clean and smart,
Speak to your Maker and open your heart.

Praise and thank Him, All day long
And say you're sorry if you've done wrong.

He'll forgive you and give you the power
To think and do good each second and hour.

13

7. Baby Amina

Baby Amina climbed up the stairs;
Baby Amina fell over some chairs.

She tumbled and rolled and started to cry,
But no one could stop her, yet hard did they try.

14

Till Sister Khadijah began saying her prayers;
Baby Amina then laughed at the chairs.

So if you're so silly to fall down the stairs,
Remember Khadijah just saying her prayers.

15

8. Three Good Boys

Three good boys,
Three good boys.
See how they pray,
See how they pray.

They pray together
in a very straight line;
And follow the *Imam* in perfect time;
They're three good boys.

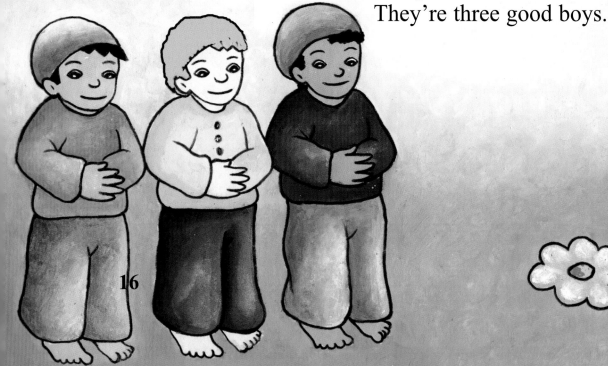

16

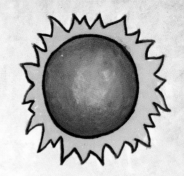

Three good boys,
Three good boys,
See how they pray,
See how they pray,

They listen and pray without any noise,
And think about Allah and not their toys;
They're three good boys,
                    Three good boys.

17

9. Fatima! Fatima! Where Have you Been?

Fatima! Fatima! Where have you been?
I've been to *Madrassa* with Nur-ud-din.

Fatima! Fatima! What did you there?
We learned to be Muslims and all about prayer.

Fatima! Fatima! When go you again?
We're going next Saturday at quarter to ten.

Fatima! Fatima! Can I come with you?
Yes, of course, you're most welcome, too!

10. Where Are You Going To, Omar Abdullah?

Where are you going to, Omar Abdullah?
I'm going to London, *Insha-Allah*

How are you going, Omar Abdullah?
I'm going by train, *Insha-Allah*.

Why are you going, Omar Abdullah?
I'm going shopping with Aisha,
Insha-Allah.

What will you buy, Omar Abdullah?
Clothes, food and toys, *Insha-Allah*.

You're a good boy, *Al-hamdulillah*.
I hope you enjoy yourself, *Insha-Allah*.

11. The Straight Path

One, two, — what I say must be true;
Three four, — my faith must be sure;
Five, six, — try not to play tricks;
Seven, eight, — my way must be straight;
Nine, ten, — help women and men;
Eleven, twelve, — for truth I must delve;
Thirteen, fourteen, — be tidy and clean;
Fifteen, sixteen, — must never be mean;
Seventeen, eighteen, — by Allah I'm seen;
Nineteen, twenty, — my provision is plenty.

22

12. Bread Man! Bread Man!

Bread Man! Bread Man!
Have you any bread?
Yes son! Yes son!
Three rolls of bread;
One for your family,
One for the school and
One for that poor old man
Who lives with his mule.

23

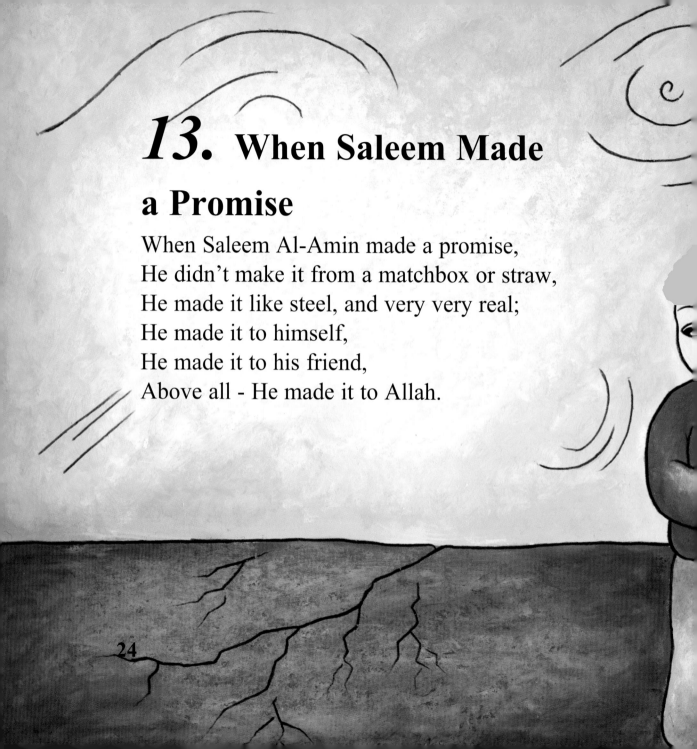

13. When Saleem Made a Promise

When Saleem Al-Amin made a promise,
He didn't make it from a matchbox or straw,
He made it like steel, and very very real;
He made it to himself,
He made it to his friend,
Above all - He made it to Allah.

24

He made it to keep, so it would never break.
Come high wind, volcano or even earthquake.

25

14. The Muslims are Coming!

La-ilaha-illal-lah
The Muslims are coming.
They've been before,
They're bringing Islam
To every door.

La-ilaha-illal-lah
The Muslims are coming
By day and by night;
They tell what is wrong,
And say what is right.
La-ilaha-illal-lah

The Muslims are coming
With a message for man;
Allah's the lord,
True guidance - Qur'an
Muhammad the Prophet,
Allah's Messenger to Man.

La-ilaha-illal-lah
Muhammadur-Rasulullah'
Allahu Akbar!

27

15. Go Forward, Young Muslims!

Go forward young Muslims
Wherever you are;
In the shadow of the sun
Or by the light of a star;
    Your Supreme Protector is
    Almighty Allah.

Go forward young Muslims,
Whoever you are;
Press forward and forward
To the light of Allah.
    And repeat and repeat,
    Al-hamdulillah!

28

GUIDES FOR THE TUNES OF Muslim Nursery Rhymes

3. **'Silver Star'** based on *'Twinkle Twinkle Little Star'*

4. **'Little Pony'** based on *'I had a Little Nut Tree'*

5. **'Adhan'** based on *'Little Boy Blue'*

6. **'Boys and Girls, It's Time to Pray'**

based on *'Boys and Girls Come Out to Play'*

7. **'Baby Amina'** based on *'Humty Dumpty'*

8. **'Three Good Boys'** based on *'Three Blind Mice'*

9. **'Fatima! Fatima! Where Have You Been?'**

based on *'Pussy Cat, Pussy Cat, Where Have You Been'*

10. **'Where Are You Going To, Omar Abdullah?'**

based on *'Where Are You Going To, My Pretty Maid?'*

11. **'The Straight Path'** based on *'One, Two, Buckle My Shoe'*

12. **'Bread Man! Bread Man!'** based on *'Baa, Baa, Black Sheep'*